W9-CFV-456
3 1668 02579 0749

CHILDRENS SMITH
796.352 SMITH
MY FIRST GOLF BOOK

My First Golf Book

by

James and Lauren Smith

Hi, I'm Chipper. Look for me on every page!

Illustrated by TuVinh Vuong

For Chelsea, Taylor, and Alexis

About the Authors

James and Lauren Smith live in Northern Virginia with their three children.
James is a PGA Professional and golf instructor at Fair Oaks Golf Park in Fairfax, Virginia.
For more information visit our website @ www.westlandgolf.com or
contact James at 703.222.6600 ext.17.

CTL Publishing
12210 Fairfax Towne Center, Suite 18
Fairfax, Virginia 22033

Printed and Manufactured in the United States by Worzalla Publishing
ISBN 0-9669116-0-1
Library of Congress Catalog Card Number
99-072074

My First Golf Book

by

James and Lauren Smith

Illustrated by TuVinh Vuong

30
20
10

Golf is a game that is fun to play.

Here is the golf course.

2
Time to tee-off!

Sand play is very important.

3
Let’s build a castle!

Sometimes it's hard to find
the golf ball.

4
Where did it go?

Ducks and geese like the pond.

5

Other animals like the golf course too.

Uh-oh! Here comes a storm.

Hurry to the club house!

SHOP

There are lots of things to see in the golf shop.

Golfing makes you hungry.

What’s for lunch?

Look at the beautiful rainbow.

Everybody back on the course!

Putting is fun. Watch the ball roll in the hole.

On a good golf day you’ll see lots of birdies and eagles.

Oops! The ball went in the water!

WOW! A hole-in-one!

14

15
The grass on the golf course needs
mowing everyday.

The sun is setting.

Our golf day is almost over.

Back to the club house.

17
Time to go home.

Nite-nite little golfers.

See you in the morning.